Happy reading —
Margaret Singleton Decker

MR. BILLIWICKET'S BURRO

Mr. Billiwicket's Burro

Ten Stories by

Margaret Singleton Decker

Illustrated by Charles J. Berger

Exposition Press   **Hicksville, New York**

First Edition

© 1959, 1960, 1961, 1962, 1963, 1964, and 1980

by Margaret Singleton Decker

Grateful acknowledgment is given to "The Christian Science Monitor" for first printing these stories.

ISBN 0-682-49565-4

Printed in the United States of America

For my parents, who would have been pleased,
and for Ralph, who is

Contents

MR. BILLIWICKET'S BURRO

Mr. Billiwicket's Burro

Mr. Billiwicket didn't mean to have a burro at all. He needed a second pony. There were so many children wanting rides in his pony cart, he decided to have two.

When he went to buy another pony there was none left. "How about a burro?" said the pony man. "I have just one left."

He brought out a burro about the size of a large dog. His coat was dull and his eyes were sad.

Mr. Billiwicket shook his head. "He's much too small for a pony cart."

"I know he's small, even for a burro," whispered the pony man. "And he isn't very handsome, either. To tell you the truth, nobody wants him."

"Maybe that's why he looks so sad," said Mr. Billiwicket. "But I can't use him. He won't be any help to me in my business."

Just then the burro touched Mr. Billiwicket's arm with his nose and looked at Mr. Billiwicket with his big, sad eyes, and Mr. Billiwicket sighed a big sigh and said, "I'll take him."

The children all petted the burro, but they soon lost interest in him because he was too small to pull them in the cart. They went back to the pony for rides, and the little burro just stood and looked sad.

"I wish I knew what to do to make you happy, Burro Baby," Mr. Billiwicket said.

Burro Baby stayed close to Mr. Billiwicket. After a while he looked less sad. He followed Mr. Billiwicket around like a dog. If Mr. Billiwicket bent over to pick flowers, Burro Baby looked over his shoulder. When Mr. Billiwicket worked on the pony cart, Burro Baby was at his heels.

"Shoo! Can't you see I'm busy?" Mr. Billiwicket always said. But he didn't really mind, and Burro Baby knew it. He would run off a way and kick up his hooves and run right back. He even had a twinkle in the eyes that had been so sad.

They played a game every evening. Burro Baby followed Mr. Billiwicket into the kitchen. Mr. Billiwicket put him out. Burro Baby peeked through the screen door. When Mr. Billiwicket wasn't looking, Burro Baby came in again and lay under the table by Mr. Billiwicket's feet. Mr. Billiwicket pretended he didn't know Burro Baby was there. He let him stay there until bedtime.

Burro Baby slept in the garage until the weather turned cold. It was even too cold for pony rides, and Mr. Billiwicket decided it was time to board the pony on a farm, where he stayed till spring.

"You'll have to go, too, Burro Baby," said Mr. Billiwicket. "Who ever heard of a burro kept in the house like a—a puppy!"

Burro Baby looked at him. The twinkle faded from his eyes and he looked sadder than ever.

The farmer was surprised to see a burro as well as the pony.

"Please take good care of them," said Mr. Billiwicket.

"I will," said the farmer.

Mr. Billiwicket drove away quickly. He should have felt happy that Burro Baby had a warm winter home with the pony and the farm animals. But when he tried to sing as he drove home alone, the tune got stuck in his throat.

At home it was strange not to have Burro Baby tagging at his heels. He missed the game of putting Burro Baby out and having him sneak in again to lie at his feet under the table.

After supper Mr. Billiwicket tried to read his paper. Every page seemed to have a picture of Burro Baby looking at him with his sad eyes. "Nonsense!" Mr. Billiwicket told himself. He went to bed. And he dreamed of Burro Baby.

When he looked out of his window the next morning, he saw the first snow of winter on the ground. He saw something else, too. Something small and furry with four legs and sad eyes, standing outside the kitchen door.

"Burro Baby!" cried Mr. Billiwicket. He rushed out and flung his arms around Burro Baby's neck.

Burro Baby rubbed his head happily on Mr. Billiwicket's shoulder.

"I missed you, Burro Baby," said Mr. Billiwicket. "You must have missed me, too, if you walked all the way back home from the farm!" He hugged Burro Baby hard. "Well, that settles it. If nobody ever before heard of a burro living in a house like a puppy, they're going to hear of it now! You can sleep right under the table, where it's warm."

The twinkle came back into Burro Baby's eyes. And they never looked sad again.

Burro Baby's Playmate

Mr. Billiwicket was on his way to the garage with Burro Baby right at his heels. It would soon be time for pony cart rides again, and Mr. Billiwicket was going to paint the pony cart. This year it would be a beautiful bright red.

Burro Baby remembered it from last summer. He also remembered how busy Mr. Billiwicket was, taking care of the pony and the cart and the many children who wanted rides. When it all began again, Mr. Billiwicket wouldn't have as much time for Burro Baby as he had had through the winter. It had been so cozy there in the big kitchen where Mr. Billiwicket let him stay, Burro Baby almost wished that the summer wouldn't come. But here it was.

In the garage Mr. Billiwicket started to paint the pony cart. Burro Baby stood as close as he could. In fact, his nose was almost in the paint bucket.

"Oops! You nearly got that brushful of paint in your ear, Burro Baby!" cried Mr. Billiwicket.

"Don't stand so close. You'd look funny with a red ear!"

Burro Baby backed away. He felt lonely already, and the pony cart rides hadn't even begun.

He wandered out into the warm sunshine and looked back over his shoulder. He hoped he would be called back, but Mr. Billiwicket was too busy stroking red paint onto the pony cart.

Burro Baby's head drooped. He was feeling sorry for himself when he saw something move under a bush near him. Then he heard a tiny sound. He walked slowly to the bush and peeked under it. He blinked his eyes at a small bundle of gray fur with blue eyes that blinked back. It was a kitten, the first that Burro Baby had ever seen.

The kitten crept out from under the bush. She looked up at Burro Baby and mewed softly. Burro Baby backed away in surprise, and the kitten followed him. She rubbed against his hoof. Burro Baby touched the kitten's small head with his nose. She rolled over, then jumped up and rubbed against his hoof again. Burro Baby decided he liked that.

Mr. Billiwicket came out of the garage with the paintbrush in his hand.

"Well, well, Burro Baby," he said, "who's your playmate?"

Playmate. So that's what this small bundle of fur was! Burro Baby ran a little way off, and Playmate pranced after him. They played and played. Burro Baby had never had so much fun.

"She must be lost," said Mr. Billiwicket as he

fixed their dinner. "I never saw her around here before. We'll have to try to find her owner, you know."

Burro Baby pretended not to listen. He and Playmate ate their dinner side by side. When it was time to go to sleep, Burro Baby curled up under the kitchen table as usual. Playmate curled up under Burro Baby's chin.

The next day Mr. Billiwicket put an ad in the lost-and-found column of the newspaper. He waited and waited, but nobody came for Playmate.

"Well, Burro Baby," he said, "I guess your little playmate can stay with us. She'll be fine company for you while I'm busy with the pony cart."

That was what Burro Baby thought, too.

He carried her on his back and played tag with her and watched over her like a father. And always she slept curled up under his chin. Burro Baby grew to love her more than anyone in the world, except Mr. Billiwicket, of course.

On the day of the first pony cart rides, Burro Baby stood watching Mr. Billiwicket and the children. Playmate sat on Burro Baby's back and watched, too. One little girl waiting in line with her father suddenly pointed at Playmate.

"Daddy," she cried, "that looks like our lost kitten!"

Mr. Billiwicket whirled around. "Are you sure?" he asked anxiously. "I put a kitten-found ad in the paper two weeks ago, but nobody answered it."

"That must have been the day our neighbor's dog ran off with our paper," the little girl's daddy

said, laughing. "We had a kitten-lost ad in at the
same time!"

"Oh, dear," said Mr. Billiwicket, "how stupid of
me! I never thought to look for *your* ad. Oh, dear
me! Then I suppose this kitten really is yours. We'll
be sorry to lose her." He sighed. "She and my little
burro have become very fond of each other, as you
can see."

They all turned toward Burro Baby. He and
Playmate looked so happy together!

The little girl ran over to pick up Playmate, but
she stopped short. She turned back to her daddy
and said, "Why couldn't we just leave her? She
looks as though she belongs here now. And we
have the other two kittens."

"That's a wonderful idea," said her daddy.
"We're glad she found a happy home. Thank you,"
he said to Mr. Billiwicket, "for taking such good
care of her."

"Don't thank me," said Mr. Billiwicket with a
big grin. "Thank Burro Baby. He takes better care
of her than I could!"

And Burro Baby was so happy he almost burst
his burro skin.

Burro Baby Goes to Work

"Burro Baby," said Mr. Billiwicket one evening, "pretty soon that kitchen table won't fit over you any more!"

Burro Baby looked up at Mr. Billiwicket from under the table. If burros smile, he was smiling.

Mr. Billiwicket laughed. "What will we do, then? Fix you up out in the garage with the pony?"

Burro Baby stopped smiling.

Mr. Billiwicket reached down and scratched Burro Baby's forehead. "Don't worry," he said. "If we have to, we'll just get a bigger table. I couldn't get along without you in here to keep me company. Both of you." He stroked Playmate's head. She was almost a cat now, but she still slept curled up under Burro Baby's chin as she had when she was only a kitten.

Burro Baby sighed contentedly and closed his eyes.

The next morning he forgot to duck and he bumped his head on the table when he came out from under it. He guessed he must be getting to be a big burro.

That was the day Playmate decided she was a cat and no longer a kitten. She didn't want to play tag with Burro Baby, or ride on his back. She sat in the sunshine licking her paws and washing her face. She acted as though Burro Baby wasn't even there. After a while she strolled around the garden, then scrambled up a tree and crouched on a limb to watch everything below.

Burro Baby gazed up at her. He was disappointed that she didn't want to play, and yet he understood how she felt. He felt a little the same way. Today, playing seemed a waste of time. Yet he didn't know what to do instead.

He wandered into the garage. The pony nodded good morning to Burro Baby and kept right on eating his breakfast. He would soon be at his important job of pulling the pony cart.

Burro Baby stood looking at him and at the pony cart. It made him wish *he* had something important to do. He walked over to the pony cart and backed up to it. He stood there dreaming of what it must be like to be hitched up and trotting around with some child in it. The more he thought about it, the better he liked it.

He was still dreaming when Mr. Billiwicket came in to hitch up the pony. He looked at Burro Baby in surprise.

"Why, Burro Baby," he said, "what in the world are you doing there? How can I hitch up the pony with you in the way?"

Burro Baby took a few steps forward, then backed up quickly to the same spot. He gazed at Mr. Billiwicket so hard his eyes almost spoke.

Mr. Billiwicket scratched his own head. Then he laughed. "Well, I do declare! You're trying to tell me *you* want to pull the pony cart?" He shook his head and put his arm around Burro Baby's neck. "You *are* growing up, Burro Baby, but you aren't big enough to pull the pony cart. Come on, now, let me hitch up the pony."

Burro Baby held back a little, but he finally let Mr. Billiwicket lead him away from the pony cart. He stood close by while Mr. Billiwicket hitched up the pony. He looked so sad that Mr. Billiwicket wished he *could* pull the pony cart.

Mr. Billiwicket thought about it all day. After the last pony cart ride, he had an idea. He said to Burro Baby, who was right at his heels, as usual, "You wait here. I just thought of something."

He went into the garage and came back very soon. He was pulling something after him. "Here we are, Burro Baby!" he cried. It was a small green wagon. "A burro cart, just for you!"

He took some leather straps out of the wagon and fixed them to make a harness on Burro Baby. He fastened one end of a rope to the harness and the other end to the handle of the wagon.

"Now pull, Burro Baby. It's very light." Burro Baby pulled. The little wagon rolled along behind him.

"That's wonderful!" said Mr. Billiwicket as he walked beside him. "You know, I had forgotten that

I was trying to buy another pony for a second pony cart the day I bought you! But there were no more ponies and you were too small. Now here we are with two carts after all!"

Burro Baby beamed. At last he had an important job to do, just like the pony!

Every day he took his place with his green wagon beside the pony with the red pony cart. Every day he trotted around the pony cart track as many times as he wanted to. And sometimes he had the very smallest customers riding in his wagon. The smallest of all was Playmate, who had decided it was still all right to play like this, even if she *was* a cat now and not a kitten!

Burro Baby Goes Skating

Mr. Billiwicket looked with sparkling eyes through the window at winter on the other side. Winter sparkled back so brightly it made Mr. Billiwicket blink. He rubbed his hands together with glee.

"I think this is the day, Burro Baby," he said. "I think this is really the day I'll try my ice skates again. I haven't had them on for years!" He hurried up to the attic to get them.

Playmate opened a sleepy cat eye and asked, "Ow?" But Burro Baby didn't know what skates were, either. Playmate closed her eye and went back to sleep.

Mr. Billiwicket was soon back. "Here they are, Burro Baby. Now let's see if they still fit me." He took off one shoe and put on one skate. "Fine," he said. "I can still wear them." He tied them together for carrying and put on his hat and coat.

Burro Baby followed him to the door.

16

Mr. Billiwicket hugged Burro Baby, but he said, "Don't you want to stay here with Playmate where it's warm and cozy? It's pretty cold outdoors. I won't be gone long. I'm just going to the pond. I just want to see if I still remember how to skate."

He hurried out the door.

Burro Baby stood thinking about skates and wishing he could see what skating was. He was still standing there when the door began to swing gently open. Mr. Billiwicket had been in such a hurry, the latch hadn't caught.

Burro Baby stepped back as a large amount of cold air came in. Playmate sneezed delicately and snuggled deeper into her chair cushion.

An open door is for going through. Burro Baby took a deep breath and stepped outside. He had to see what skating was.

His small hooves tinkled on the hard road as he trotted to the pond. He remembered the way and didn't get lost once. He and Mr. Billiwicket and Playmate had been there many times on picnics.

It looked different now. He stood on the snowy bank and watched people of all sizes gliding on the pond like birds in the sky. So that was skating!

He saw Mr. Billiwicket on the far side of the pond, gliding along like a bird, too. Burro Baby thought it looked like fun. He wondered if he could do it. He had no skates, but his hooves were hard and smooth. They should slide very well.

They did. He put one of them onto the frozen pond and the next moment all four legs flew out from under him. He found himself sprawled in a most unburrolike way all over the ice.

He tried to scramble back onto his legs, but the more he tried the more they kept going in every direction except under him, where they belonged. He finally gave up and just stayed where he was, feeling silly. He thought everybody was looking at him.

Mr. Billiwicket glided over to him and kneeled down beside him. "Oh, my, oh, my, Burro Baby, are you all right?" he asked worriedly.

Burro Baby tried to hide his head under Mr. Billiwicket's arm. But he wiggled all his legs and his tail to show he was all right.

Mr. Billiwicket patted him sympathetically. "It makes you feel mighty foolish, doesn't it, Burro Baby? But you should have seen *me* today, when I first tried my skates. Oh, my! I had to be helped up four times before I could stay up."

Burro Baby peeked out from under Mr. Billiwicket's arm.

"It's a fact, Burro Baby. Everybody falls down sometimes."

A small boy wobbled past them and suddenly sat down hard.

"See what I mean?" Mr. Billiwicket helped the small boy up. Then he helped Burro Baby up and steered him back to the snowy bank.

"I'm afraid skating isn't for you, Burro Baby. Too many hooves to take care of."

Burro Baby looked so sad, Mr. Billiwicket said, "Oh, dear me, there must be *some* way."

The small boy wobbled over to the snowy bank and plopped down on the toboggan he had left there. Suddenly Mr. Billiwicket had a happy-thought look. "Would you rather ride on your toboggan?" he asked the boy.

The small boy nodded.

"Mind company?"

The small boy grinned and shook his head happily. He helped Mr. Billiwicket settle Burro Baby on the toboggan; then he got on board behind Burro Baby. Mr. Billiwicket took the rope and skated across the pond, pulling the toboggan.

He went faster and faster until at last Burro Baby, too, was gliding like a bird in the sky. He wasn't actually skating himself, but he thought it was wonderful.

So did Mr. Billiwicket. The rest of the winter he took Burro Baby and a toboggan with him every time he went skating. But they always closed the door carefully so Playmate could stay warm and cozy.

Burro Baby and the Stranger

It was warm and cozy in Mr. Billiwicket's kitchen until the door opened. Besides a blast of cold air, a Christmas tree blew in, with legs at the bottom and a head at the top.

"Well, well, Merry Christmas, little ones," cried Mr. Billiwicket, who really owned the legs and head. "Now we can trim the tree and be ready for Christmas."

Burro Baby and Playmate, the cat, shivered under the kitchen table until the door was closed again. They watched Mr. Billiwicket sleepily. It seemed strange to have a tree *inside* the house, but if Mr. Billiwicket wanted it there, it must be all right.

Mr. Billiwicket hummed "Jingle Bells" as he hung lights and ornaments and icicles all over the tree.

Burro Baby dozed. When he opened his eyes again he stared at the tree. It glowed and sparkled and twinkled as no outdoor tree ever did, not even after an ice storm. *This* glow and sparkle was all colors.

Mr. Billiwicket was rocking in his rocking chair and reading the Christmas story aloud to himself. Burro Baby liked to hear it, too, although he didn't know exactly what it was about. He also liked Mr. Billiwicket's kitchen, all cozy inside while winter banged and whistled outside trying to get in. But it couldn't. There were just Mr. Billiwicket and Playmate and himself—and the beautiful tree.

Suddenly Burro Baby heard something besides Mr. Billiwicket's voice. It was a soft whimpering outside the door. It could hardly be heard over the voice of the winter wind, but soon Mr. Billiwicket heard it, too. Then there was a scratching on the door.

"My goodness, Burro Baby, what can that be?" said Mr. Billiwicket. He jumped out of his rocking chair and opened the door.

A thin dog with big eyes and a small tail stood shivering on the doorstep.

"Well, come in, stranger, come in!" said Mr. Billiwicket. "It's no night to be out there."

Burro Baby pulled farther in under the table. He didn't like cold air coming into the cozy kitchen. He didn't like this strange dog coming in, either, but Mr. Billiwicket was treating him like a special guest. He rubbed him with a towel to warm him up and fed him with a leftover hamburger. The stranger ate it as though he hadn't had one lately.

Burro Baby watched with a feeling he had never had before. He didn't like Mr. Billiwicket fussing

over this stranger. Mr. Billiwicket belonged to him and Playmate. There was a cold lump somewhere inside Burro Baby.

Mr. Billiwicket looked over at him. "Don't you want to come over and make friends?" he asked. Burro Baby didn't move.

"Oh," said Mr. Billiwicket, as though he knew about the cold lump. "Well, maybe later."

He patted the floor near the stove and said to the stranger, "You sleep right here. We'll take good care of you until we can find out where you belong."

The stranger wagged his tail and licked Mr. Billiwicket's hand. Mr. Billiwicket patted Playmate and Burro Baby good night, but Burro Baby didn't lick his hand.

Burro Baby woke often through the night. Every time he opened his eyes, he could make out the shape of the stranger curled up all alone and still shivering once in a while.

Then Burro Baby had a dream. He and Playmate and the stranger were in a place like a barn, with a cow and a donkey and a sheep. There were a man and a woman and a tiny baby. And all around there was a glow even more beautiful than Mr. Billiwicket's Christmas tree. Burro Baby was feeling very sorry for the stranger. In fact, he thought the stranger was a very nice dog indeed.

It was a nice, warm feeling. It was where the cold lump had been.

Burro Baby woke up, startled. Something touched his side. It was the stranger. He was curling up under the table near Burro Baby and

Playmate. When he saw that he had wakened Burro Baby, he quickly moved away.

Playmate woke, too. She arched her back, but instead of spitting or clawing she strolled over and rubbed her head under the stranger's chin. Then she said, "M-m-m," and went back to sleep.

Burro Baby wondered if he was still dreaming. He still felt sorry for the stranger, and the warm feeling was still inside him where the cold lump had been. Not only did he think the stranger was a very nice dog, but he was thinking how nice it would be if the stranger could stay with them.

He touched noses gently with the stranger, who sighed happily and settled under the table close to Burro Baby and Playmate.

That's how Mr. Billiwicket found them Christmas morning. "Well, well," he said, beaming, "it looks like a very Merry Christmas—and not just this one Christmas day!" He looked at the stranger. "You seem to be a welcome stranger," he said. "Let's call you 'Welcome.' 'Welly' for short."

Burro Baby stuck his ears up straight. Playmate said, "Prrrrurp!" And Welly almost wagged his small tail right off, he was so happy.

Burro Baby's Almost Picnic

Burro Baby stepped outside Mr. Billiwicket's kitchen door. Cat Playmate was right behind him, and behind her came Dog Welly.

They all took deep breaths of early spring. Their noses wiggled happily as sunbeams and small breezes tickled them.

Mr. Billiwicket was digging the earth in his window box so it would be ready for spring planting.

"I wonder if I should plant some pink geraniums instead of red ones again this year," he said to nobody in particular.

Burro Baby came up behind him and touched him with his nose. Mr. Billiwicket looked around and smiled.

"Pretty nice day, isn't it, Burro Baby? It won't be long until we can have our first picnic by the pond."

Burro Baby wished they could have their first picnic this very day. He pressed his forehead hard against Mr. Billiwicket, then turned and ran a little way. He stopped and looked hopefully.

Mr. Billiwicket laughed and shook his head. "It's not quite picnic weather yet, Burro Baby. We'd find it much colder out by the pond than it is here, and it wouldn't be much fun."

Burro Baby's ears drooped. It felt warm enough to him. It had been cozy in Mr. Billiwicket's kitchen all winter, but it wasn't the same as the warm sunshine. Mr. Billiwicket just wanted to dig in his old window box. That was why he wouldn't go on a picnic this beautiful day.

A bird sang in a tree close by and seemed to agree it was a *perfect* day for a picnic.

The more Burro Baby thought about the pond, the more he wished for that picnic. He thought about it so much that by afternoon he decided he just had to go to the pond.

Mr. Billiwicket was having a nap. Welly had gone off somewhere. Cat Playmate wouldn't wake up from her own nap, no matter how much Burro Baby poked her, so he went by himself. Nobody saw him go.

It seemed farther than usual to the pond. He hadn't gone there alone since the first time he ever saw it frozen solid—with Mr. Billiwicket skating on it. Traveling was more fun with company.

When he reached the pond, the sun had gone under some clouds and the air felt like winter again. There were small, cold patches of snow here and there.

The pond was ruffled and shivery-looking. Burro Baby walked to a flat rock at the edge. He stood on it and looked out over the water, dreaming about picnic time.

Suddenly the flat rock he was standing on gave a loud C-R-A-C-K! He was so startled he nearly fell off. Then he realized the rock was moving. In fact, it wasn't a rock at all, but a piece of ice that had broken away from the shore and was rocking gently in the ruffled water.

Burro Baby was adrift on a small raft made of ice.

He was afraid to move, even to look over his shoulder. The breeze was stronger than it had been, and it seemed to be pushing his raft away from shore.

He didn't know how big the pond was or how far he might drift on it. He didn't know whether or not he could swim if he had to; he had never tried. He wished he was safely back under Mr. Billiwicket's kitchen table, smack in the middle of winter.

He looked down at his raft and thought it looked smaller around the edges. Could it be melting? What would he do if it melted right out from under him?

Burro Baby closed his eyes. He couldn't think of anything else to do. He began to tremble so hard he shook the raft.

Then he heard sounds from the shore behind him. A loud MEOW! That sounded like Playmate. A loud RIFF! That sounded like Welly. A loud "Burro Baby, what are you doing out there? Come back!"

That sounded like Mr. Billiwicket.

Burro Baby forgot about tipping the raft if he moved. He started to turn around to look at the shore, and with a loud splash he landed in the pond —sitting on the bottom. But he landed facing shore, and he was right: there stood Playmate and Welly and Mr. Billiwicket.

When Burro Baby scrambled to his hooves, the water came up only to his knees. It was shallow, but cold enough to be twenty feet deep. He waded to shore.

Welly riffed and riffed as he bounced around Burro Baby. Playmate rubbed and rubbed against his cold, wet ankles. Mr. Billiwicket hugged and hugged him.

"Oh, Burro Baby, we were so worried about you!" he said. "Then I remembered how much you wanted to go on a picnic. We hoped you were at the pond, but we didn't expect to find you *on* it and *in* it!"

He took a carrot out of his pocket and gave it to Burro Baby. "There," he said, "that's almost a picnic!"

Burro Baby was feeling very cold, but he rubbed Mr. Billiwicket's arm to say thank you. And he was first in line on the way to their warm home to wait a little longer for spring and picnics.

Mr. Billiwicket's Medium-Wild Duck

Mr. Billiwicket liked to look through his kitchen window first thing every morning. He also liked to be sure that something cheerful looked back at him in case the sun didn't. That's why every spring he planted red geraniums in his kitchen window box.

Burro Baby watched him smooth the fine dark earth and give it a final pat under the last red geranium.

"There we are, Burro Baby," Mr. Billiwicket said with pride. "All planted. This is the finest boxful we've ever had." He said that every spring, and every year they *did* seem to be the finest.

The next morning Mr. Billiwicket went straight to the kitchen window to look at his red geraniums. He gasped so loudly at what he saw that he woke Burro Baby.

"My goodness, Burro Baby, we have something in our window box besides geraniums!"

31

Burro Baby opened a sleepy eye and came out from under the kitchen table. When he looked through the window he opened both eyes wide. The window box held a strange-looking flower all right; it had feathers instead of petals.

"A wild duck, I do declare!" cried Mr. Billiwicket. "Well, medium-wild duck."

The duck turned her head and looked right into Mr. Billiwicket's eyes. She didn't seem afraid. She settled herself more cozily among the geraniums and closed her eyes.

"Oh, my!" said Mr. Billiwicket. "It looks as though Mother Mallard has decided to nest in our window box and hatch her ducklings right in the middle of our geraniums! We must make sure she isn't disturbed or upset."

That wasn't easy. The news got around that Mr. Billiwicket had a medium-wild duck in his window box, and everyone came to see her.

Mother Mallard didn't mind. She even appeared to enjoy being the center of attention as long as nobody came too close. Especially Playmate, the cat. But one poke from Mother Mallard's strong bill taught Playmate to do all her duck-watching safely behind the window.

Soon there were six eggs under Mother Mallard. Mr. Billiwicket looked out many times a day to see if they had hatched.

One morning when he looked out, the window box was full of geraniums and broken eggshells, but no Mother Mallard. And no ducklings. Just one dark feather.

"They've hatched and gone, Burro Baby," said Mr. Billiwicket sadly, "and we never even had one peek at them."

He took the broken eggshells out of the window box and carefully saved the feather.

For the next several days he thought about Mother Mallard and the ducklings.

"I wish we could see them," he said to himself one day as he tended to his geraniums. "I'll bet they look mighty cute paddling around after their mother." He almost dropped the trowel. *"Paddling around!"* he echoed loudly. "The pond! Of course, that's where Mother Mallard would take them, so they could be handy to it when they got their waterproof feathers and could swim."

He hurried into the kitchen, with Burro Baby at his heels. "We're going on a picnic, to see those ducklings," he said as he packed peanut butter sandwiches and apples and a few carrots in the picnic basket.

They hurried to the pond.

The willow boughs were wearing misty, green scarves. The sky was wearing bright, white cloud puffs. Violets were hiding so shyly in the grass they almost got stepped on.

"Things look different now from the way they did in the winter when we came to skate, don't they, Burro Baby?" Mr. Billiwicket asked, laughing.

Burro Baby skidded a little just remembering.

He and Mr. Billiwicket looked out over the pond. A breeze was decorating it with tiny ripples. Something else was decorating it, too.

"Here they come!" cried Mr. Billiwicket. He and Burro Baby met them at the shore. Mother Mallard quacked happily, and the six newly feathered bits of ducklings tried to make noises of welcome, too. Mr. Billiwicket and Burro Baby shared their lunch, but there wasn't nearly enough to satisfy everybody. Mr. Billiwicket and Burro Baby were still hungry when everything was gone. The ducklings scrambled right into the picnic basket looking for more bread.

"We'll come back often," Mr. Billiwicket promised as he tipped the ducklings out of the basket, "and we'll bring lots of bread for your share."

Mother Mallard quacked a thanks-we'll-be-waiting.

Burro Baby looked back at the Mallard family as he and Mr. Billiwicket walked away. Then he looked into the empty picnic basket and up at Mr. Billiwicket.

Mr. Billiwicket laughed. "Yes, Burro Baby. Next time you and I will eat part of our lunch at home before we come here for a picnic with our medium-wild ducks!"

Burro Baby and the Painting

"It's picnic time, it's picnic time,
We're happy as can be—
Burro Baby, Playmate Cat,
Welly Dog and me!"

Mr. Billiwicket chanted on their way to the pond.

Playmate and Welly chased each other. Burro Baby and Mr. Billiwicket followed more slowly, but Burro Baby kicked up his heels in sheer joy. Even Mr. Billiwicket did a little jig. It was a heel-kicking, jig-dancing kind of day.

Half the people in town thought so, too. There were dozens of them having picnics at the pond. Mr. Billiwicket and his four-footed family had to walk halfway around it before they found an empty spot big enough to spread the picnic blanket on and stretch all their fourteen legs.

"Ahhhhhh," said Mr. Billiwicket. Playmate and

36

Welly sat down beside him to wait. They knew that the first thing he always did was to look at the pond for a while. And it would probably be longer than usual today because just then Mr. Billiwicket spied Mother Mallard, the medium-wild duck, and her ducklings heading for shore.

"Hello there, Mother Mallard!" cried Mr. Billiwicket. "My, my, haven't the ducklings grown!"

The Mallard family came up to Mr. Billiwicket, quacking their greetings.

"I won't forget you at lunchtime," Mr. Billiwicket promised, "but it isn't time yet." He shooed them back into the pond, but they didn't go far away.

Burro Baby wandered farther along the shore. On the other side of a big clump of bushes a large lady was seated on a small folding canvas stool. In front of her was a wooden rack called an easel, and on the easel was an almost-picture.

"Oh, dear," sighed the lady as she dabbed at it with her brush.

Burro Baby came up behind her and looked over her shoulder. She leaned back and squinted. Burro Baby leaned forward and peered. That was when the lady noticed him.

She shrieked and drew away so far that she tipped over. She dropped her palette of paints on the ground, paintside down, of course, like buttered bread.

Burro Baby was so startled himself that he turned and somehow backed sideways smack-dab into the wet painting. The lady was on her knees picking up her spilled things. She looked up and saw the smeared picture.

"Oh, you—you little *donkey!*" she cried.

Burro Baby didn't know what to do. He hung his head and felt foolish. The lady got back onto her feet just as Mr. Billiwicket came rushing around the bush with Playmate and Welly at his heels.

"Oh, my, Burro Baby!" he exclaimed as he saw what had happened. "Did you do that?"

"Is that—that donkey yours?" the lady asked. She looked ready to cry.

"Yes, but he's really a burro," said Mr. Billiwicket, "and I'm sure he meant no harm. We're terribly sorry."

"I know," sniffed the lady. "It was an accident." She blew her nose and tried to smile. "We were both surprised, that's all. But look at my picture! I'll never get it right for the art exhibit now."

Mr. Billiwicket shook his head. "And look at my Burro Baby!" he said. "*He* should be entered in the art exhibit instead!"

Burro Baby was a sight, with a big splotch of paint on one side. Both Mr. Billiwicket and the lady couldn't help laughing, but they also patted Burro Baby, so he knew they weren't really making fun of him.

"Will you let us share our picnic with you to show you how sorry we are?" Mr. Billiwicket asked the lady. He told her his name and introduced Playmate and Welly. She had already met Burro Baby.

"Thank you, that would be lovely," she answered. "I'm Mrs. Doodledummer, but everybody calls me

Auntie Doodle because I love to doodle with paints."

She poured some turpentine on a cloth and cleaned the paint off Burro Baby. "There now," she said, "we're ready for lunch."

When the picnic basket was empty—and there had been plenty for everyone, including the Mallard family—Auntie Doodle said, "How nice this has been, meeting you all! I'm even glad the painting was spoiled. I never win a prize, but it's fun to enter the art exhibit anyway."

Burro Baby was standing quietly near her. He hadn't taken his eyes off her, and they were trying to tell her how sorry he was about her picture. His eyes were also telling her how nice she was and that, after Mr. Billiwicket and Playmate and Welly, he liked her better than anybody in the world.

At last Auntie Doodle's eyes met his. She stared and understood every thought he was thinking.

"Burro Baby!" she cried, inspired. "I'll paint a picture of *him* for the art exhibit!"

She got right to work. Everybody kept still, Burro Baby the stillest of all. After a long time Auntie Doodle said, "Now I can finish at home, and the paint will be dry by day after tomorrow, for the exhibit."

They all went home to wait for day-after-tomorrow. It finally arrived, and Mr. Billiwicket hurried as soon as he could to see the picture of Burro Baby.

Everyone was gathered around one picture with a "First Prize" sign above it. Mr. Billiwicket joined the crowd to look at it.

He rubbed his eyes. He knew he had left Burro Baby at home, but here he was, looking as real as at the picnic, right inside the frame.

Auntie Doodle was beside the picture, beaming like sunshine. "Sorry," she kept saying, "it isn't for sale."

"Oh, dear," said Mr. Billiwicket, "I'm sorry, too. It's the best picture of Burro Baby that could ever be. I wish I might buy it."

"But it will be yours as a gift as soon as the exhibit is over," Auntie Doodle said merrily. "That's why it isn't for sale. It's my thank you to you and Burro Baby for helping me find out what I can paint best. And don't thank me!"

So Mr. Billiwicket didn't, just then, but only because he couldn't find his voice to thank her.

Burro Baby Goes to the Fair

It was a beckoning day.

"Burro Baby," said Mr. Billiwicket at breakfast, "we've been working hard. I think we'll take the day off from selling pony- and burro-cart rides and do something special. Wait till I do the dishes, and we'll all go to the fair. Everyone will be there anyway."

Burro Baby didn't know what a fair was, but anything Mr. Billiwicket wanted was fine with him. He went out with Cat Playmate and Dog Welly and stood sniffing.

The air was so full of perfume even a bird remarked, "Sweet!"

Playmate rubbed against Burro Baby's ankles. Welly woofed at a squirrel scampering past. It seemed to be taking Mr. Billiwicket a long time to wash the dishes.

Then in the distance they heard faint music. Come-and-see-sounding music. They turned their heads to listen, and before they knew it they were traveling in that direction.

The music led to the edge of town. It grew louder, and Mr. Billiwicket's little family met more and more people heading the same way, talking about the fair.

So the music was calling, come-to-the-fair! And there they were—the great Ferris wheel, candy booths, snap-the-whip, the balloon man, and all the rest. The music was coming from the merry-go-round.

Burro Baby went up to the crowd of children waiting to get on. They all knew him.

"Come on, Burro Baby! *You* ride for a change!" they cried.

Burro Baby wasn't sure he wanted to get on that big, round platform with the wild-looking ponies on it. They were going up and down on poles, instead of trotting sedately as Mr. Billiwicket's pony did.

When the merry-go-round stopped, Burro Baby sniffed cautiously at one of the ponies.

It smelled like wood and paint! Well, there was nothing to fear from a wooden pony.

He stepped onto the merry-go-round. A boy immediately climbed onto his back. He was pretty heavy to sit on a small burro, but Burro Baby only turned and looked at him with big brown eyes.

The merry-go-round began to move. Burro Baby's eyes grew bigger and rounder. The merry-go-round went faster. Burro Baby couldn't remem-

ber ever traveling that fast before, and *never* in a circle.

The boy on his back jiggled up and down with excitement and drummed his heels on Burro Baby. It didn't really hurt, but it wasn't much fun, either. Burro Baby wished he had waited for Mr. Billiwicket. After a long time the merry-go-round stopped. A second boy climbed on Burro Baby the minute the first one got off.

Nobody seemed to think Burro Baby minded. He acted as gentle as ever, but he began to think he wasn't ever going to get off that merry-go-round. He wondered what Playmate and Welly were doing.

Playmate was having her own adventure. She had climbed into a chair on the Ferris wheel when it was standing still, but now it was moving. Playmate went clear to the top of the Ferris wheel.

She was higher than in any tree she had ever climbed. She yowled to get down, but nobody heard her above the other noises.

Welly was lost among all the legs walking around. He was far from the merry-go-round and the Ferris wheel.

He had licked up some ice cream a little girl had lost from her cone, but now he didn't know what to do or which way to go.

At that moment a big shoe that didn't know where it was stepping came down on Welly's toes. The crowd was so thick Welly couldn't run, so he sat down and howled.

When Welly put his mind to it, he could out-howl any dog in town. His heart was in it now. The merry-go-round music stopped for a moment, and over all the other sounds of the fair came the very un-fairlike sound of an unhappy Welly.

Burro Baby heard it, and he jumped off the merry-go-round just as the fourth little boy was about to get on him. He pushed through the crowd in the direction of Welly's howl.

Playmate heard it just as she reached the ground again. She jumped off the Ferris wheel and wove around and between feet to get to Welly.

Mr. Billiwicket, just entering the fairground, heard it and hurried as fast as he could. He and Burro Baby and Playmate reached Welly at the same time. So did half the folks at the fair.

Welly stopped howling when he saw his family and wagged just as hard as he had howled.

"Oh, my," said Mr. Billiwicket, "what have you all been up to? You should have waited for me."

They couldn't tell him that any more than they could say how they wished they *had* waited. Burro Baby went a few steps and looked back.

"Ready to leave?" Mr. Billiwicket laughed. "Wait till I buy us some hot dogs and cookies and pop, and we'll take them to the pond for a picnic. The fair is fun, but I guess we'd like to go somewhere quieter now, wouldn't we?"

Burro Baby and Playmate and Welly all wagged their tails and crowded close to Mr. Billiwicket. It was the only way they could tell him how right he was—they weren't going to be more than two steps away from him for the rest of the day.

Mr. Billiwicket's
New Year's Eve

Mr. Billiwicket gazed out through the window at the last day of the year. It even looked like the tag end of something: raggedy twigs, thin patches of snow, and ice with holes in it.

Mr. Billiwicket sighed and went over to switch on the lights of the little Christmas tree. It was losing a lot of needles, but it still twinkled merrily.

He thought of the year that would end at midnight. What a nice year it had been, and how he would miss it! It had brought them many happy times, like the picnic at the pond, when they met Auntie Doodle painting and she did a portrait of Burro Baby.

Mr. Billiwicket sat down in his rocking chair. Burro Baby came and rested his head on Mr. Billiwicket's knee. Cat Playmate climbed up onto his shoulder and rubbed against his ear. They knew how he felt, as animal friends always do. Dog Welly

sat at his feet and looked up at him with big, sympathetic eyes.

This time last year, Welly was a "Welcome Stranger," but not a stranger for long. Welcome he would always be.

Mr. Billiwicket patted them absently. His mind was on time and how fast the years go by. And none had ever gone as fast as this one had.

The room was so quiet he could hear tiny ticks as more needles from the Christmas tree hit the floor. He sighed so loudly he shocked himself right out of his chair and Playmate off his shoulder.

"Tut, tut," he scolded himself, "this won't do at all! The little new year won't feel welcome here if I keep thinking of the old one! I'll make us some fudge, that's what I'll do."

He bustled about, mixing and stirring. The kitchen began to smell gloriously like a candy shop. By the time he poured the fudge into the pan to harden, Mr. Billiwicket heard himself whistling.

"That's more like it," he told himself.

He set the pan outside the door to cool. As he straightened up, someone called, "Happy New Year, Mr. Billiwicket!"

"Auntie Doodle!" he cried. "What a surprise! Come in!"

"Just for a minute," chirped Auntie Doodle, coming up the walk. In one hand she carried a basket bulging mysteriously under a cloth cover. Under her other arm she carried a big, flat package. "I can stay only long enough to unload!"

They went inside, and everybody crowded

around to welcome her. She set the package and basket on the table. First from the basket came a big, white pet-store bone tied with a red ribbon. "This is a kind of birthday gift for Welly," she said, "because he began a whole new life with you about this time last year, didn't he?" Mr. Billiwicket nodded. "And aren't we glad he did!"

Next came a box of catnip for Playmate. And a bag of carrots for Burro Baby. And last, a splendid chocolate cake with one pink candle in the center.

"Every birthday needs a cake," Auntie Doodle said. "Welly won't mind sharing his with the new year!"

Then she handed Mr. Billiwicket the big, flat package. It was wrapped in willow-green paper and tied with a buttercup-yellow ribbon that looked like spring.

"Oh, my!" said Mr. Billiwicket as he opened it carefully. If it was spring on the outside of the package, it was summer on the inside. He stared at a painting of the picnic at the pond when they had met Auntie Doodle. They were all in it, even the medium-wild ducks. And Auntie Doodle, painting!

She beamed at the look on his face. "I did two and thought you'd like one. It may remind you of a happy time this year."

"Oh, *thank you!*" said Mr. Billiwicket at last. "It's beautiful. I'll think of happy times to come *next* year when I look at it, too."

"Well, I must be off," said Auntie Doodle, pick-

ing up her basket. "We're having company tomorrow, and I'm not ready! Happy New Year!"

"Happy New Year to you, too, and many thanks,"
said Mr. Billiwicket as she went out.

He sprinkled some of the catnip for Playmate.
She rolled in it with delight. He gave Welly the bone.
Welly's tail wagged so fast it was a blur.

Burro Baby accepted one of his carrots, munch-
ing it under the kitchen table as he watched Mr.
Billiwicket hang the new picture beside the one of
Burro Baby.

Then Mr. Billiwicket lit the candle on the cake,
and the whole room seemed to glow with the tiny
flame. That was when he noticed something under
the cake plate. He moved the cake and saw a seed
catalog with a burst of red tulips on the cover. He
chuckled softly. That Auntie Doodle! For her it was
spring already!

He chuckled louder. Why, his own new seed
catalog would be arriving soon, with spring right
on its heels. Time flew, just as he had been thinking
earlier!

He looked out of the kitchen window and could
almost see red geraniums in his window box!